THIS BLOOMSBURY BOOK

BELONGS TO

....

To Henrietta and Rosemary,
both of whom have helped me so much
MN

For all the children and teachers
at Lilliesleaf Primary School
PB

BLOOMSBURY
CHILDREN'S
BOOKS

First published in Great Britain in 2002 by Bloomsbury Publishing Plc
38 Soho Square, London, W1D 3HB
This paperback edition first published in 2003

A CIP catalogue record of this book is available from the British Library

ISBN 0 7475 6119 2

Printed in China by South China Printing Co.

5 7 9 10 8 6 4

Mole and
the Baby Bird

by Marjorie Newman

illustrated by
Patrick Benson

BLOOMSBURY
CHILDREN'S
BOOKS

Mole found a baby bird. It had fallen out of its nest.

Mole waited and waited but no big bird came to help it,

so Mole took the
baby bird home.

He made a nest for it.
"Look, Mum!" he said.

"It's very, very hard to take care of a baby bird," said Mum.

"They usually die," said Dad.
"My bird won't die," said Mole.

His friends helped him find food for the baby.

Mum showed him how to feed it.

Mole fed it whenever it chirped.
And the bird didn't die. It grew!

"It's my pet bird," said Mole.
"It's not a pet bird. It's a wild bird," said Mum.
The bird fluttered its wings.

"Your bird is trying to fly," said Mum.
"No!" cried Mole. "It mustn't fly!"

Mole found some wood and some nails.

He borrowed Dad's toolbox.

"What are you making?"
asked Dad.

"I'm making a cage for my pet bird," said Mole.

"It's not a pet bird.
  It's a wild bird," said Dad.
"You should let it fly."

"No!" cried Mole.

He put his bird into its new cage.
The bird was sad.

Mum was sad, too.
But Mole kept his bird, because he loved it.

Then Grandad came to visit.
He looked at Mole's pet bird.

Presently Grandad said,
"Let's go for a walk, little Mole."

Grandad took Mole to the top of a high hill.

Mole looked down at the trees far below.

He felt the wild wind trying to lift him.

"Wheee! I'm flying!" cried Mole.
"Nearly," said Grandad.

When Mole got home he looked at his bird.

It was sitting very still in its cage
in Mole's dark underground room.

"Birds are meant to fly," said Mole.

He opened the cage door and he let his bird fly away,
because he loved it.
Then he cried.

Next day Mole went into the forest.
He saw his bird flying, soaring, free.
And Mole was glad.

Acclaim for *Mole and the Baby Bird*

'a sure-fire classic for children of all ages' *Publishing News*

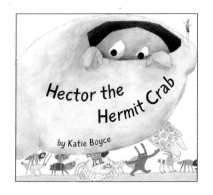

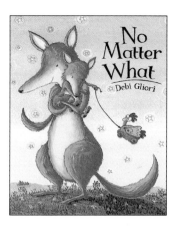

HECTOR THE HERMIT CRAB
Katie Boyce

MARVIN WANTED MORE
Joseph Theobald

FRAN'S FRIEND
Lisa Bruce & Rosalind Beardshaw

NO MATTER WHAT
Debi Gliori